FRED PUDDING

Anne Vittur Kennedy

Albert Whitman & Company
Chicago, Illinois

Today we are making
Fred Pudding.
It's so good.

I'm Fred.
I know how to make it,
so watch me.

First, get stuff.
All kinds.

Next, grease the pan.
The cat is unnecessary.
Don't worry about him.

Next, shred some of
the stuff into chunks.

Like this,

and this,

and this.

Get out of the heat and cool it a little while.

Make some sauce.

Stir it up good.

Garnish.
That just means add
a pretty decoration.
Like this!

Voilà!

Fred Pudding!

So good.
Let's make it again tomorrow!

Fred's Bread Pudding

PUDDING STUFF:

- 24 slices of bread (about 1 1/2 loaves),
- French brioche, challah, raisin bread, cinnamon bread, or any combination of these
- 5 large eggs
- 1 stick butter, melted
- 1/2 cup light brown sugar
- 1/2 teaspoon cinnamon
- 1/2 teaspoon nutmeg
- 1/8 teaspoon salt
- 1 tablespoon vanilla
- 2 cans (12 oz. each) evaporated milk
- 1/2 cup raisins (optional)

TOPPING STUFF:

- 1/2 teaspoon cinnamon
- 1/2 cup sugar
- 1/4 cup butter, softened
- Several vanilla wafer cookies, coarsely crushed
- 1/3 cup chopped pecans

SAUCE STUFF:

- 1 cup powdered sugar
- 1 tablespoon heavy cream
- 1 tablespoon vanilla
- Whipped cream for garnish

1. Preheat oven to 350 degrees. Grease 9" x 13" pan or dish.

2. Shred bread into chunks and place in large mixing bowl. Set aside.

3. Combine butter and brown sugar in a small bowl and stir until the sugar dissolves.

4. Add eggs to another large bowl and beat with a whisk. Next add cinnamon, nutmeg, salt, and vanilla and stir. Then add the butter and brown sugar mixture to the bowl. Pour in the evaporated milk and stir until smooth.

5. Pour the egg-and-milk mixture over the bowl of bread chunks. Make sure all the bread is coated. Press the bread down into the mixture lightly and let it soak.

6. While the bread is soaking, make the topping. Add the cinnamon and sugar to a small bowl. Crumble the butter, cookies, and pecans into the bowl, and mix with your hands until all the ingredients are combined into a crumbly mixture.

7. Transfer half of the soaked bread mixture to the greased pan. Top with raisins if desired, then add the rest of the bread. Sprinkle the topping over all.

8. Bake at 350 degrees for 40–50 minutes until lightly browned and puffy. Remove pudding from the oven and let cool while you make the sauce.

9. Combine the powdered sugar, cream, and vanilla to make a simple vanilla frosting. Add warm water as needed to make the frosting a thinner sauce, then drizzle the sauce over the pudding. (The sauce can be warmed a little in the microwave if you'd like.)

10. Serve the bread pudding warm. Add a little more sauce to each serving if needed. Garnish servings with whipped cream.

VOILÀ!

For Carter

Library of Congress Cataloging-in-Publication Data

Names: Kennedy, Anne, author, illustrator.
Title: Fred pudding / words and pictures by Anne Vittur Kennedy.
Description: Chicago, Illinois: Albert Whitman and Company, 2018.
Summary: "While Grandma and her grandson make bread pudding in the kitchen,
Grandma's tubby dog Fred makes 'Fred pudding.'"—Provided by publisher.
Identifiers: LCCN 2017061616 | ISBN 978-0-8075-2581-4 (hardcover)
Subjects: | CYAC: Bread puddings–Fiction. | Cooking–Fiction. | Dogs–Fiction.
Classification: LCC PZ7.K3768 Fre 2018 | DDC [E]–dc23
LC record available at https://lccn.loc.gov/2017061616

Printed in China
10 9 8 7 6 5 4 3 2 1 WKT 22 21 20 19 18

Design by Morgan Beck

For more information about Albert Whitman & Company,
visit our website at www.albertwhitman.com.